Grena and the Magic Pomegranate

Grena and the Magic Pomegranate

BY MELVIN LEAVITT

ILLUSTRATED BY BETH WRIGHT

Carolrhoda Books, Inc./Minneapolis

Carolrhoda Books, Inc. c/o The Lerner Group
241 First Avenue North, Minneapolis, MN 55401

LIBRARY OF CONGRESS CATALOGING-IN-PUBLICATION DATA

Leavitt, Melvin.
  Grena and the Magic Pomegranate / by Melvin Leavitt ; illustrated by Beth
Wright.
    p.   cm.
    Summary: After healing the Fireling prince's sick child, Grena receives a
magic pomegranate bush.
    ISBN 0-87614-760-0
    [1. Fairy tales. 2. Pomegranate—Fiction.]
I. Wright, Beth, ill. II. Title.
PZ8.L4752Gr   1994
[E]—dc20   92-7850
                                                   CIP
                                                    AC

Manufactured in the United States of America

1 2 3 4 5 6 – I/JR – 99 98 97 96 95 94

For Alton and Zelma Leavitt.—M.L.
For Bill.—B.W.

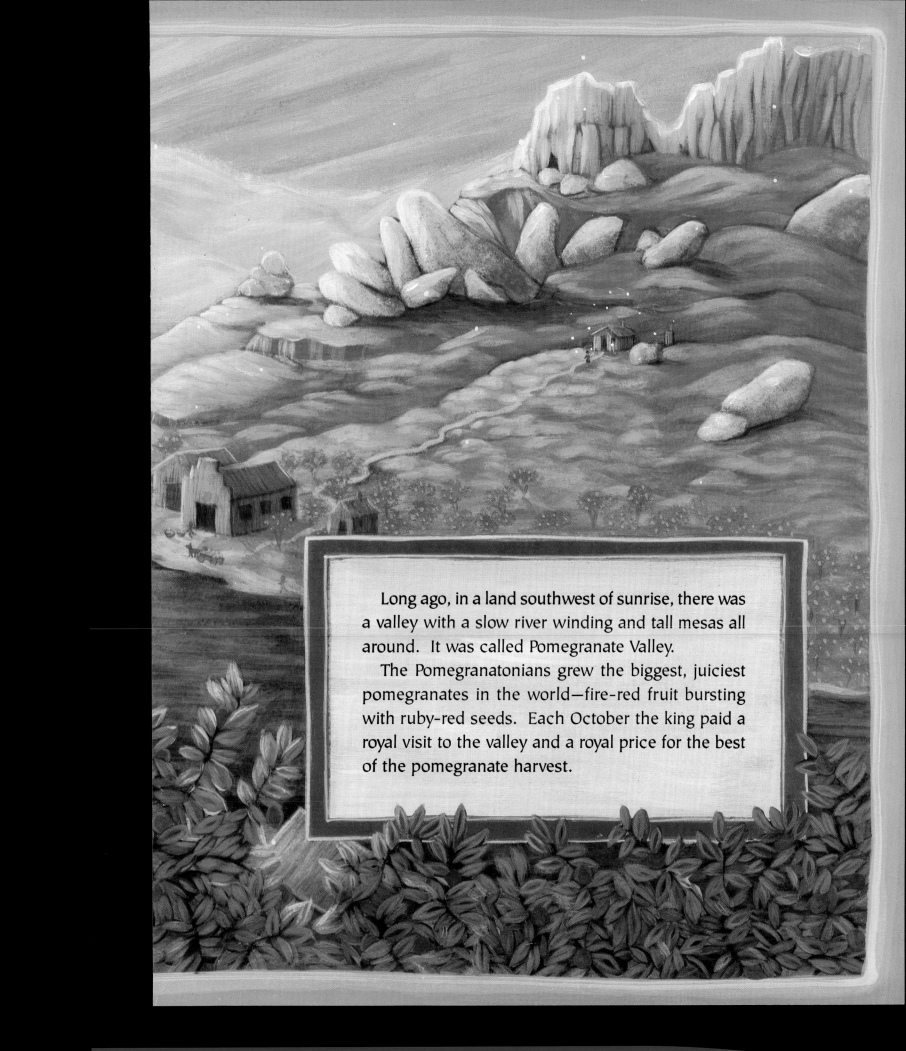

Long ago, in a land southwest of sunrise, there was a valley with a slow river winding and tall mesas all around. It was called Pomegranate Valley.

The Pomegranatonians grew the biggest, juiciest pomegranates in the world—fire-red fruit bursting with ruby-red seeds. Each October the king paid a royal visit to the valley and a royal price for the best of the pomegranate harvest.

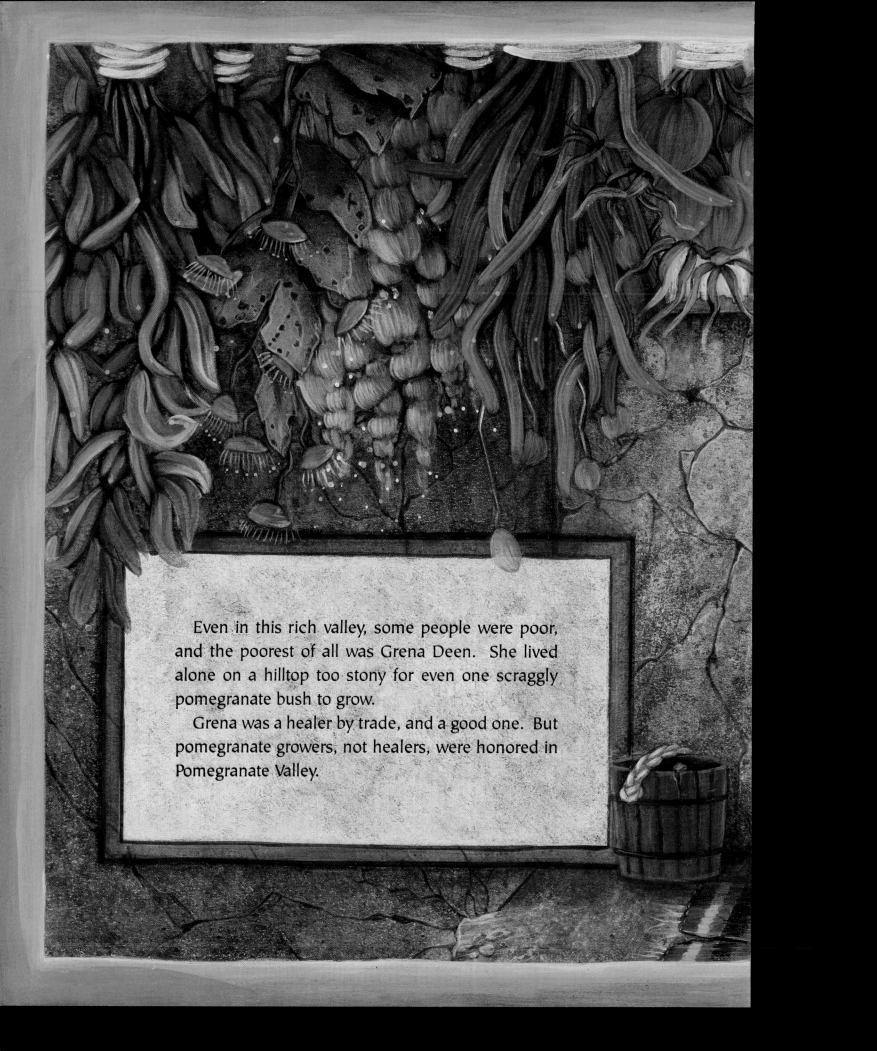

Even in this rich valley, some people were poor, and the poorest of all was Grena Deen. She lived alone on a hilltop too stony for even one scraggly pomegranate bush to grow.

Grena was a healer by trade, and a good one. But pomegranate growers, not healers, were honored in Pomegranate Valley.

One night in early spring, Grena was awakened by a loud knocking. She opened her door, and there stood a Fireling prince. She stepped back in alarm. Firelings were magical creatures, and wise people had nothing to do with them.

The Fireling's ugly face was twisted with fear, and he wrung his long fingers. "My daughter is dying!" he wailed. "Please help her!"

"Wh-what can I do?" Grena stammered. "If your magic can't save her, how can I?"

"She is beyond magic," the Fireling wept. "But there are things more powerful. I felt your kindness and wisdom far away in my castle of stone. Please come!"

Grena wrapped a threadbare shawl about her shoulders. Gathering up a few medicines, she followed the Fireling into the night. A tall horse waited, and they rode swiftly away.

They galloped a long time under the stars. At last they stopped before two gigantic boulders carved in the forms of strange beasts. Between them, Grena glimpsed a land that had haunted her dreams since childhood—the Canyon of Fire. It was a wilderness of tortured shapes. Writhing up from the earth in towers and pinnacles, blood-red stone shimmered like frozen flame. Here the Firelings lived. No human had ever entered their land and returned to tell of it.

The Fireling prince blindfolded Grena. "It is safer for you not to see too much," he said. Grena's heart pounded against her ribs.

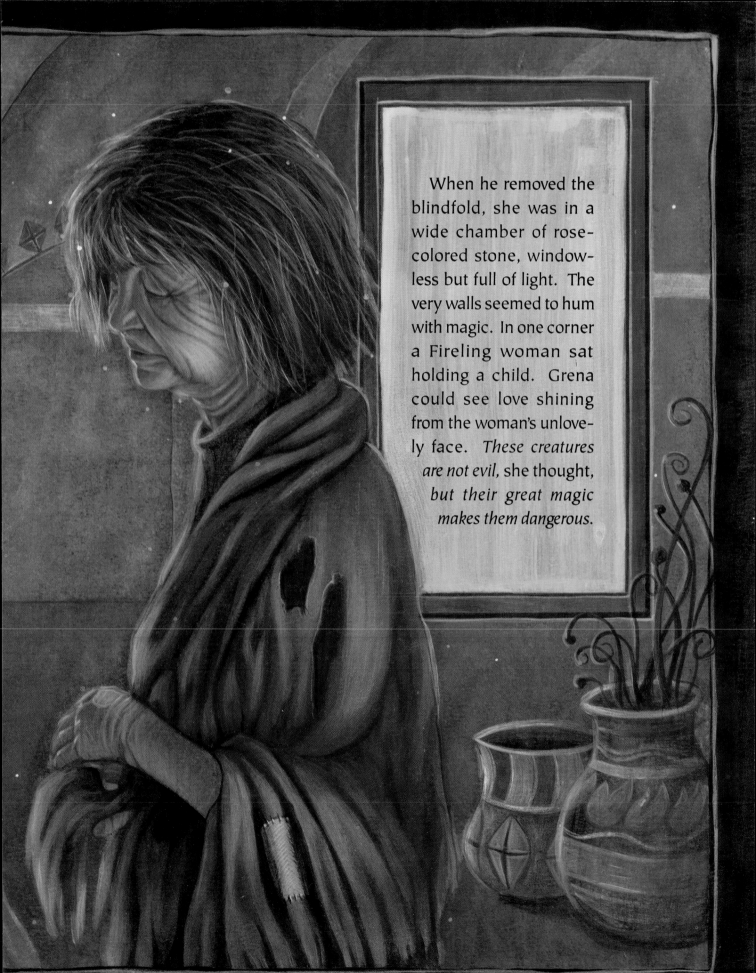

When he removed the blindfold, she was in a wide chamber of rose-colored stone, windowless but full of light. The very walls seemed to hum with magic. In one corner a Fireling woman sat holding a child. Grena could see love shining from the woman's unlovely face. *These creatures are not evil,* she thought, *but their great magic makes them dangerous.*

Grena took the child in her arms. The tiny girl was icy hot and burning cold. Her little heart fluttered weakly. Grena held the child close and tried to see what ailed her. Slowly a picture of the illness formed in Grena's mind. She saw a great, horned death-beast, dark and shining and deadly, and she understood. This was good magic gone crazy, magic out of control. And all the mighty wizardry of Fireling healers had only fed the beast.

Now the magic must be lured from the child. But how? Grena left the little one with her mother and took from her pack a jar of healing pomegranate juice. She cleared her mind, made it as pure and unmagical as the blood-red liquid. She poured juice on her palms and rubbed it into the soles of her feet.

She took the child in her crimson hands. Instantly, the deadly magic flowed into Grena. It seared through her like hungry fire, passing from her feet into the living stone. Everything before her eyes turned red, and then, suddenly, went black.

She awoke on a stone bed. The Fireling prince and his princess stood nearby. The prince held a young pomegranate plant in an earth-filled pot.

"The child..." Grena said.

The Fireling woman smiled. "She will live."

The Fireling prince drew near and handed Grena the plant. "Take this with our thanks," he said. "Plant it on your hill, and it will bear fruit this very season. But beware! Fireling gifts are dangerous and often cause more mischief than good. Promise me that you will neither eat nor sell the first harvest, but give it to me."

Grena looked doubtfully at the plant. "I promise, but it doesn't matter. Nothing will grow in my soil."

"It will grow," the Fireling said. "Water it well, both with river water and your own tears. You will not lack for either."

The prince's words proved true. Prying eyes and gossiping tongues do not sleep, and Grena had been seen entering the Canyon of Fire. When she returned home, the Pomegranatonians called her "Fireling-lover" and "witch woman" and spoke to her only with insults. She planted the pomegranate bush and carried water from the river each day to slake its thirst. And she shed many a tear.

The Pomegranatonians came in crowds to jeer at her. "Go live in the Canyon of Fire with your friends!" they yelled. They would have pulled up her little bush and burned it if they dared, but no one was brave enough to touch a Fireling gift. Worst of all, they would not let her tend the sick, and it pained her to see anyone suffer when she could have helped.

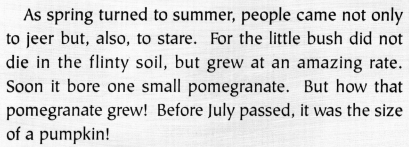

As spring turned to summer, people came not only to jeer but, also, to stare. For the little bush did not die in the flinty soil, but grew at an amazing rate. Soon it bore one small pomegranate. But how that pomegranate grew! Before July passed, it was the size of a pumpkin!

By September, it could have filled a washtub, and it was so heavy that Grena had to prop it up with boards. It was bright scarlet and perfectly round. The Pome-granatonians' greed overcame their fear, and they offered Grena great wealth for the bush. They knew the king would pay a fortune for this pomegranate.

But Grena, poor though she was, remembered her promise and refused their offers. Poverty and loneliness went with her to the river many times each day. But she kept her vow to water the bush well, and it was now the largest in the valley.

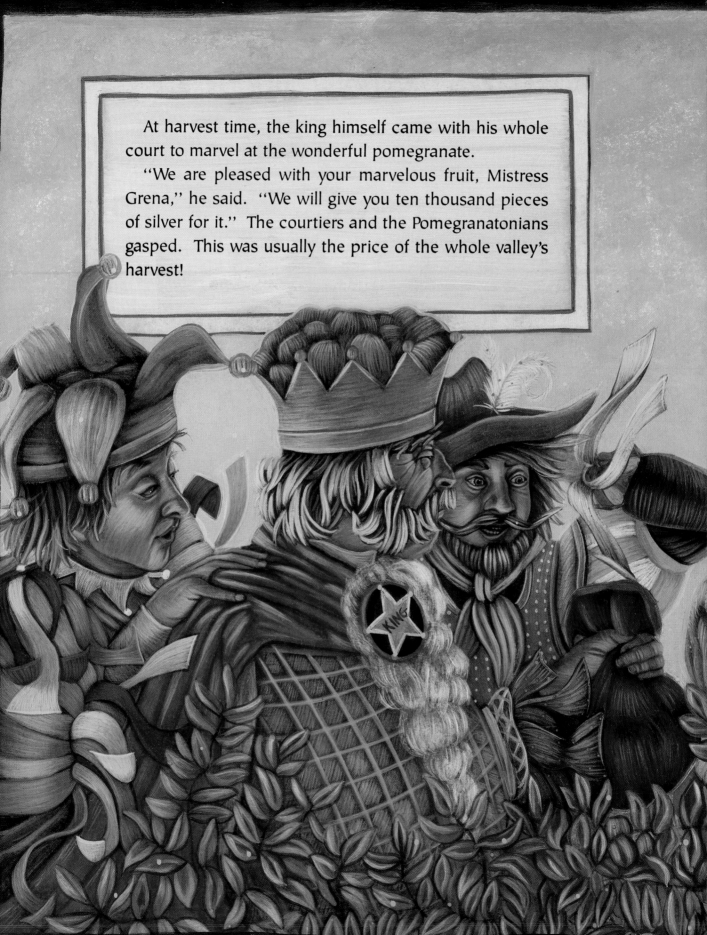

At harvest time, the king himself came with his whole court to marvel at the wonderful pomegranate.

"We are pleased with your marvelous fruit, Mistress Grena," he said. "We will give you ten thousand pieces of silver for it." The courtiers and the Pomegranatonians gasped. This was usually the price of the whole valley's harvest!

Tears came again to Grena's eyes. She was so poor and so hungry and so tired of everyone being angry at her.

"I'm sorry," she said in a small voice, "but I have promised the first fruit to someone else."

The king was furious. "What?" he bellowed. "And who in this kingdom comes before the king?"

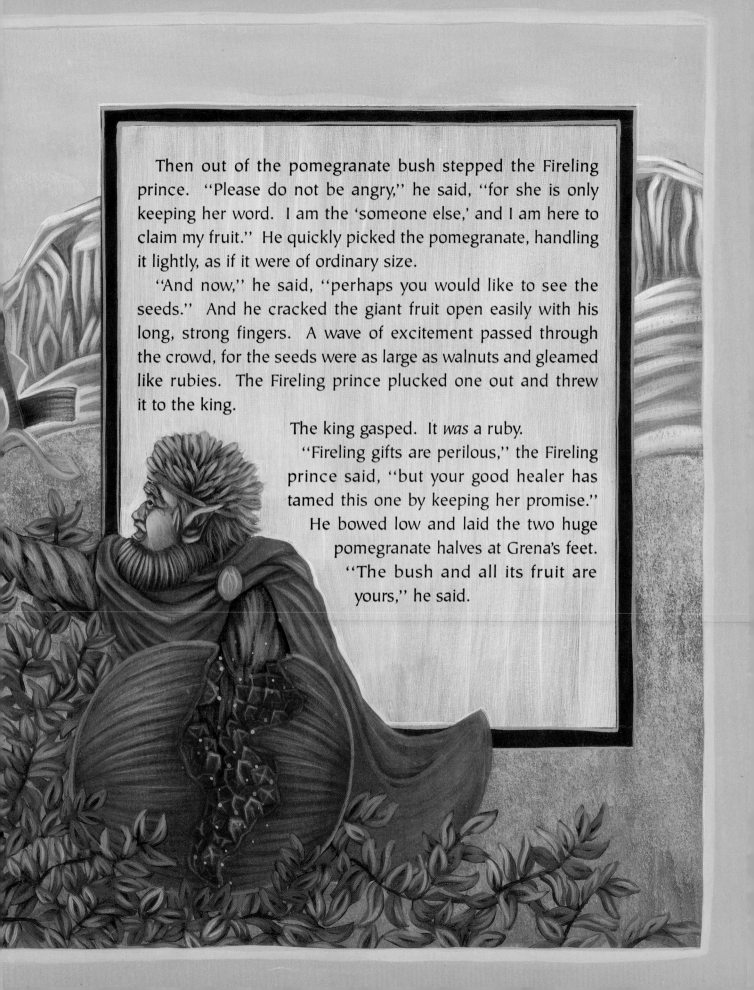

Then out of the pomegranate bush stepped the Fireling prince. "Please do not be angry," he said, "for she is only keeping her word. I am the 'someone else,' and I am here to claim my fruit." He quickly picked the pomegranate, handling it lightly, as if it were of ordinary size.

"And now," he said, "perhaps you would like to see the seeds." And he cracked the giant fruit open easily with his long, strong fingers. A wave of excitement passed through the crowd, for the seeds were as large as walnuts and gleamed like rubies. The Fireling prince plucked one out and threw it to the king.

The king gasped. It *was* a ruby.

"Fireling gifts are perilous," the Fireling prince said, "but your good healer has tamed this one by keeping her promise." He bowed low and laid the two huge pomegranate halves at Grena's feet. "The bush and all its fruit are yours," he said.

Grena built a cottage where her hut had been and used the rest of her rubies to help the poor. Her bush grew so large that it became a tree, and every year it produced a pomegranate bigger than the year before. But Grena healed the sick—human and Fireling alike—and lived in peace and joy, never giving her heart to riches.

Grena, the Firelings, and the Pomegranatonians have all passed from the earth. But you can still find the flames of stony fire in a land southwest of sunrise. And in a valley nearby, with a slow river winding and tall mesas all around, pomegranates still grow to this very day.